MISSION ACROSS...

A Sci-fi Thriller Navigating the Multiverse

by

Dr. Siddharth Gupta

MBBS, MS (Ortho), DNB, MNAMS
Goldmedalist, FIAA (England)

Published by:

F-2/16, Ansari road, Daryaganj, New Delhi-110002
☎ 23240026, 23240027 • *Fax:* 011-23240028
info@vspublishers.com • www.vspublishers.com

Online Brandstore: amazon.in/vspublishers

Regional Office : Hyderabad
5-1-707/1, Brij Bhawan (Beside Central Bank of India Lane)
Bank Street, Koti, Hyderabad - 500 095
☎ 040-24737290
vspublishershyd@gmail.com

Follow us on:   

BUY OUR BOOKS FROM: AMAZON FLIPKART

ISBN 978-81-978303-6-5
New Edition

Printed at : Param Offsetters, Okhla, New Delhi–110020

Foreword

Dr. Siddharth Gupta, the surgeon (Primary facet) is a bold man, hard working who meticulously prepares all of his planned surgeries. He very well knows about the requirements and put all his efforts towards achieving the same.

Dr. Siddharth Gupta, the administrator (Secondary facet) came to force when we opened our own Hospital, *Adarsh Multispeciality Hospital & Trauma Centre.* A complete team man, keeping organisation before self. Never shy away of hard talk or bold decision which is in favour of the organisation be it pushing co-directors or staff. You are bound to learn something or the other everyday in his company. His discipline is infectious and you can only respect that. He is the man who can walk the talk. He managed to do Post Graduate Diploma in business management when not a minute was available for self and family.

Dr. Siddharth Gupta, the author (Tertiary facet).

Firstly, I wonder how could he manage time for it. Then I realized an artist under his skin was keen to make his own way and finally did it. He penned down a novel which if you start reading will not be able to get up once you finish it. He beautifully unfolded the complexities of multi-dimensional universe along with the matter and mankind, thereby explaining and fixing the social responsibility we have.

This novel is a must read for an individual of any age, group or profession. It takes you to a journey of exploring your unimaginable potentials. It makes one realize how a common individual can play his/her role in the society for its betterment. The story is based on an evolving scientific principle. Meanwhile the story takes some romantic turns which eventually leads the characters to unleash the unsolved mystery of a bridge which had become notorious for mysterious road accidents.

– Dr. Dheeraj Kumar Singh
MBBS, MD (Medicine)
Consultant Physician

Preface

Being a meticulously blessed surgeon can be one of the most precious gifts that a devotee can ask from his almighty. I am blessed to have learned the skill of saving lives of the mankind with utmost precision. I am blessed that I have a family that I can count upon in my bad times and celebrate during the good ones.

My attitude towards life changed drastically during the second wave of the Covid 19 pandemic. I had been an active participant in my hospital treating the patients affected with the deadly virus. There were times when even the best efforts made were futile and could not save lives. It was the time when I realized that as a doctor it might be fair to execute what you are trained for but as a human being one has to sometimes go out of the ways to do the unconventional tasks; to save the mankind and help the needy selflessly. Sometimes one might think that its not his/her duty or not a part of his/her key responsibility area to get to the core of a social problem, that is affecting millions in the world but not him/her personally. One should always remember that today its them but tomorrow it can be us. The very existence of oneself is justified if and only if s/he realizes and performs well in the character that the cosmos has sent oneself for.

The story in this book inspires three doctors to get to the core of a mysterious accidental epidemic. They solve a problem which is not a defined task of their profession but definitely a part of their humanity. This story revolves around an evolving but interesting scientific principle. Love is an impetus to realize one's dreams. The main character of the story gathers strength from his love. His love empowers him to do the impossible; which appeared beyond the capabilities of a common man.

I owe the success of this book to my parents (Mr. *Anil Kumar Gupta* and Mrs. *Sunita Gupta*) who have inspired me to bring out the best version of myself and *Sant Baba Neemkaroli*.

I dedicate this book to my daughter *Kaaira* and son *Shravil* who have always made me realize that their father is a superhuman with extraordinary abilities. I am grateful to my wife *Bhawna* who took care of our children well when I was busy writing this book in my off duty hours. I am grateful to my brother *Sudhanshu* who gifted me a new laptop which ultimately made it easier for me to complete my work.

Disclaimer: This is entirely a work of fiction. The resemblance of this story with dead or living will be purely coincidental.

PS: *A glossary is provided at the end of this book with definitions of the technical terms and key concepts. Please refer to it for better understanding and a smooth reading experience.*

Contents

The Miraculous Escape

It was a dark winter Friday night when I was returning to my home from the City Hospital, where I work as a Senior Resident Doctor in the department of orthopaedics, after the most exhaustive day I have ever had. While driving home through the roads of Delhi at 11 pm, I was half dead because of the chaotic day. The voices and mumbling of the patients were still echoing in my mind. My job seemed thankless to the hundreds of patients whom I see every day, not because I was not doing justice to my work but because of the pathetic working conditions in a few government hospitals like ours. I could not forget an old man staring at me with a nasty glance in his eyes, when I got up from my seat for just five minutes to attend the nature's call.

"Well it is all part of public dealing", I said to myself and almost shaken by the loud horn of the truck which just crossed in front of my car as I was sloping down the *Sharda* Bridge. I stopped my car by the roadside to see where the truck came from and vanished in fractions of seconds when there was no sign of it in my rear view mirror. Initially, I thought it was because of the dense smog in Delhi that I could not see it in my rear view mirror but then if it were because of the smog, how is it that it was not even there in my rear view mirror or how could I miss the shimmering of its headlight. I was only trying to understand and calculate the speed and time relationship of that giant vehicle with a dreadful horn, when I received a call

from my younger sister, *Bharti*. I took her call as my car was still parked by the roadside with parking lights on.

Samrat startled by the loud horn of the truck

"How long will you take to return home," she asked.

"Another fifteen minutes," I replied.

I resumed driving thinking I had a miraculous escape from an accident, when I saw the Delhi Traffic Police Slogan at the next traffic signal which read, "Speed thrills but kills."

I reached home with drooping eyelids and voraciously hungry. I opened the door with the duplicate key. *Bharti* and *Amaira* (my one year old niece) had already slept by then. My mother was in a deep sleep in her room and my elder brother and his wife were working on their laptops. I wish I could share the day with someone but it was too late. I quickly had my dinner lying on the dining table, without even putting it inside the microwave for a few seconds. I was starving so I decided to have it the way it was.

The Worry Begins

The next day I got up had a quick breakfast prepared by our house maid. Everybody, except for my mother and our maid, was still asleep as it was Saturday which is a holiday for both my sister and my brother, as they work in IT sector in their respective multinational companies. I wish I could be one of them when it comes to Saturday, but then all other days it's vice versa. Something to feel proud of myself that I save lives everyday and people want to be like me. After all being a healer that too as a surgeon appears to me the biggest addiction of all kinds. As I was combing my hairs I heard my mother praying from the *pooja* room when she suddenly stopped and said, "Shut the door when you leave."

I started my new car which is still in a brand new condition, even after 6 months of purchase because I maintain it that way. I got it financed from a nationalized bank after I started earning a regular salary; when I joined as a senior resident doctor about eight months back. A regular source of income is all that a bank needs as a means of financial security to sanction a car loan.

It was a light day to start with until 10 am when I received a call from the casualty about a road traffic accident victim; who was brought to our hospital by the Police Control Room (PCR) Van of the Delhi Police. I rushed to the casualty within minutes of receiving the call and took my junior resident along with me. The victim was a young male of about 24 years of age, who met with an accident early morning at about 6 am; when his Motor bike had a head on collision with a trailer near ISBT *Kashmere Gate* on *Sharda* bridge. The victim had a head injury and was drowsy. He could barely tell his name and mumbled, "It was not there before I took the turn. It appeared suddenly from nowhere. Believe me doctor it was certainly not there before." Without paying much attention to what the boy was saying I examined his blood pressure, pulse and respiratory rate. Every vital parameter was within normal limits which gave me a sigh of relief, atleast momentarily. I examined him further for any fractures or obvious injuries but he seemed to have primarily a head injury only; for which a neurosurgeon had already examined him and was doing the needful.

While I was completing the formalities of a medico legal case by completing the documents, the cop on duty started telling me something that seemed weird. He said, "Sir, the accidents near the *Sharda* bridge over the *Yamuna* river have tolled four folds this year."

"That might be because of the smog," I replied.

"The smog is there every year sir, and this time it's even less," he added.

"Then what do you think might be the possible cause of these increasing accidents," I asked him in a casual but inquisitive tone.

"Sir, I don't know exactly but something unexplained is happening near this bridge, the vehicles meet with accidents and one of the vehicles involved vanishes without leaving any trace behind it." Mr. *Yadav,* the constable replied and left due to an alert on his wireless set.

I was taken aback by the description he gave, I could feel my palpitations, my sigh of relief was not there anymore and my hands were drenched in sweat.

Constable Yadav with Dr. Samrat

What I saw last night was indeed a part of these accidents taking place, that truck also appeared and vanished within no time when I was driving back home last night across *Sharda* bridge near *Kashmere Gate*. It was not a miraculous but perhaps the most fortunate escapes I have ever had, I then recalled what that boy was mumbling while he was drowsy, "Doctor, it was certainly not there before."

The Tip of the Iceberg

I rushed to the neurosurgery ward to meet that victim who had a motor bike accident he was taken to the neurosurgery operation theatre by then.

I used to travel daily through that bridge, hence my curiosity to know about the cause of the increasing number of accidents on that particular road increased.

The reason could be anything or perhaps nothing. And definitely, it was not my job to find it out, but I could be one possible victim in near future.

Every incident taking place in our society bears a direct or an indirect correlation with our life and most of us become an ostrich by closing our eyes to it unless it; has really to do something to us personally. I was no exception to this notion that every single individual has also I was more concerned about myself. I had to take that bridge while returning home and coming back to work the next day. The only days when I was not driving in the evenings were when I was on 24 hour round the clock duty.

While I was lost in my imaginations I heard a voice calling me from the back, "Are you joining us for the lunch, Sir?" That was Dr. *Karan,* our post graduate student but more of a colleague and friend.

While we were heading towards the mess, he was telling

about the spoiled mood of the Head of the Department in the morning due to the heavy work load that winter. *Karan* got a bad scolding from him that morning. He was disappointed and was smoldering like a half burnt coal. When he noticed that I was not listening attentively to what he was saying he added, " Sir! what happened? You seem to be in your own different world today."

"Nothing" I replied.

We sat at the table for lunch and my co senior resident Dr. *Rajendra* also joined. *Karan* was peaceful by now.

Samrat, Rajendra and Karan meeting for lunch in mess

I too came out of my thoughts atleast temporarily. *Karan* was showing us his engagement ring. He got engaged to a gynecology post graduate student last week itself and returned from his leave a day before only. Early morning he got a scolding. Certainly not a good day to start with, especially when one is back from an auspicious vacation.

"Well, did you all notice that the trauma and accident cases have taken a heavy toll this winter?" asked *Rajendra*.

"Yes" both I and *Karan* replied simultaneously.

My silence that day was related to *Rajendra*'s question only, but the concern was different.

I told them what the policeman told me in the morning about the increased road traffic accidents on the *Sharda* bridge in the last month since the winters have set in. Since ours was a tertiary care hospitals near that site, we had the maximum number of cases being brought to us by the Police Control Room van. I told them my worry about myself. I even told them how I had the most fortunate escape last night and what that accident victim was mumbling, who was there in the neurosurgery operation theatre at that time.

Karan said that my botheration is not justified as such incidents do have high rate of occurrence sometimes, they follow a waxing and waning course. But *Rajendra* said that we should go to the police room in our hospital for complete information on the statistics because, he also had a tough time doing overtime duties in last couple of weeks owing to such incidents. He said that he had visited the maximum number of mortality in the last couple of weeks and he was also perturbed about these incidents.

We went to the police room and met the constable on duty. We discussed with him about the *Sharda* bridge. The moment we began he almost burst into tears and said that he had not been able to return home for last two nights; as he had been escorting the victims from *Sharda* bridge to various hospitals. Well, we asked him about the census. To our surprise, our hospital had received only fifty percent of the total cases, the rest were being managed by various secondary care hospitals. So, the magnitude of the problem was larger than our expectation. We were only seeing the tip of the iceberg.

The Search Begins

All of us (I, *Rajendra* and *Karan*) decided to visit all the secondary care hospitals, with Mr. *Yadav*, the constable, to collect the actual details and data about the accidents.

We left from the city hospital after the day's work, and started visits to the various government hospitals in the vicinity. We asked the doctors on duty in the casualty of every single hospital that we visited and inquired about the road traffic accidents cases; that were brought to the respective hospitals. To our surprise, our city hospital has catered to not more than fifty percent of the cases. The rest of the cases were being managed by the smaller hospitals in the peripheral area. Well now we were sure that something or the other is terribly wrong with that bridge over the *Yamuna* river. Mr. *Yadav*, the constable said, "Sir, can we please leave now, I want to go home and take some sleep."

We dropped Mr. *Yadav* to his home and left for our homes as well. I parked my car in the hospital campus and preferred to take a metro instead because I was scared to take that road.

I did not think about the events that happened with me day before, we rarely get off on Sundays for ourselves. So, I decided to go out for a movie with *Chandani* (my girlfriend) who is a pathologist in our hospital. We are supposed to tie the knot in next couple of months. It was a sunday well spent with her after an exhaustive week. We did not discuss about the incidents at the *Sharda* bridge. Instead, we talked about the lovely weather, our future, marriage plans and honeymoon. We had the most delicious lunch at a fine dining restaurant in *Mehrauli*. It was a memorable date amidst the unfortunate events that we had been going through.

The Factual Analysis

The next day I finished my OPD on time and decided to analyze the facts with my colleagues that we had collected from various hospitals about the rising number of road traffic accidents on *Sharda* bridge.

We worked out a few patterns in those incidents. Most of the incidents took place during the dawn and the dusk, that is, when there is a transition from night to day or day to night. A collision otherwise, involves two or more vehicles but in all those cases there used to be just one and only one vehicle involved, the other one invariably went missing. All the victims were mumbling strangely about the mysterious events that preceded the accident,when they were brought to the hospital.The other vehicle did not leave even its traces at or after the time of collision. A car colliding with another virtual car seems imaginary and fictional. *Karan* looked bewildered and was looking at both his right and left hand with his neck swaying like a pendulum while he deliberately clapped both his hands against each other. I smiled gently as I could; I understood what he was trying to figure out. Exactly the same was going through my mind too.

The lunch time was over by then.We had to get back to our post lunch workshops.

While I was still preoccupied in my thoughts I saw *Karan* talking with his fianceé who used to be his girlfriend until last

week. Courtship period gives you a dopamine surge which is even more powerful than a weed puff. Well, he was fortunate enough to get married to a girl whom he loved; unlike many others who could only dream about it and end up losing their love sooner than later. A true love goes away without warning but when it goes it no longer leaves you the same person that you were before. Its strength can make you do things that one cannot even dream of. Sometimes, I really feel the strength that the loss of true love has left inside me. Perhaps that strength is the impetus behind my curiosity to get to the core of this accidental epidemic. An epidemic with perhaps no vaccination so far. An epidemic, which is non contagious but certainly fatal. While I was lost in my thoughts I heard a voice at the top of its note in the announcement system of the hospital, "Dr. *Samrat* (myself) report to the ER immediately." The silence inside me broke like a glass with a crackling sound inside me, I knew it was another one.

I and *Karan* rushed to the ER, looking at each other with pale faces and eyes wide open.

The Unexpected Encounter

She was a young lady in her late twenties lying semiconscious in the emergency bed. She was wearing a light pink *salwar suit* with a white *dupatta* which was stained in blood and partly covered her face. I got closer to her bed and called the chaperone so that I could examine her meticulously. I slowly uncovered her face by dragging the *dupatta* off her face.

It appeared as if an important but incomplete chapter of my life just flashed in fraction of a second. She was my ex girlfriend *Shanaya,* my first love whom I lost because of some unavoidable circumstances in the past. Everything flashbacked in my mind within few seconds.

She was injured but looked simply as beautiful as she used to be a decade ago. I never imagined that I would see her in such a painful situation after such a long time. The cosmos was perhaps testing my professional skills as to how would I face it when my beloved is lying wounded on the couch. It seems that the same cosmos forgot that we are trained to keep service before self. I was numb although transient only.

Flashback-1

It was a fine pleasant day post *Diwali* in the month of November almost a decade back from that day when we met for the first time at the fest of my medical college. I was the programme coordinator for the group dance competition event. *Shanaya* was doing the last minute rehearsal with her dance troupe in the green room while she suddenly realised that her prop, a metal trident was missing. She left it in her bus which was parked in the campus approximately more than half a mile from the auditorium. She looked extremely worried and almost sulked.

Being the programme coordinator I asked her if I could help her. We heard the announcement, "The next performance, Delhi Arts College." Her worry got worsened and she turned pale. I read placard on her costume which read DAC. She gave me the bus number and asked me if I could get her the prop from the parking. I rushed like a thunderstorm and messaged the announcer to get a short interlude performance done for two minutes. I reached the parking within 30 seconds and began searching for the bus. She told me it's the red one. I finally found it and the banner of DAC assured me that I was correct. The door was locked from inside, driver looked drunk and was sleeping. I banged the windshield with a wood staff borrowed from the parking watchman and fortunately I did not end up breaking it. The driver opened the door with his eyes turned red. He badly smelt of liquor. I ignored all that, got into the bus and there it was the metallic trident. I grabbed it with both my hands and reached the auditorium before the interlude performance was over. *Shanaya* took a sigh of relief as I handed over the prop to her. She gave mesmerising performance and the auditorium echoed with the sound of applause. The curtain was drawn and suddenly a soft and touching voice with a blushy giggling tone said, "Hey, doc! Thanks a lot." I turned back, smiled and gently shrugged my shoulders and said, "Anytime madam!" She said, "I am *Shanaya,* second year student from DAC."

Shanaya (centre) with her dance troupe

I introduced myself as *Samrat Oberoi,* third year MBBS student and the programme coordinator for this event. We had fun after the event, enjoyed the rides and finally said good night when I escorted her to the bus in the parking. As she peeped out of the window of the moving bus I wondered that I am missing something, oh no! Her contact number.....? She smiled, while she waved good bye to me and pointed towards the pocket of my shirt. I tapped my pocket and felt something inside, it was a small chit with a mobile number, I looked at her again, she smiled and then the bus slowly disappeared. I immediately saved her number.

Leaving Love Behind Duty

I recouped myself, examined *Shanaya* for any major injuries. She had a concussion, she was slightly drowsy, had a cut on forehead, abrasions on both hands, bleeding gums and swelling in the right knee. She was moaning and whining in pain. I began her first aid, injected a painkiller and tetanus toxoid. I then took her to the minor OT with *Karan* and the Chaperone and stitched her wound under the local anaesthesia. I then cleaned and dressed the abrasions. After giving intravenous fluids she opened her eyes slowly and saw me standing by her side.

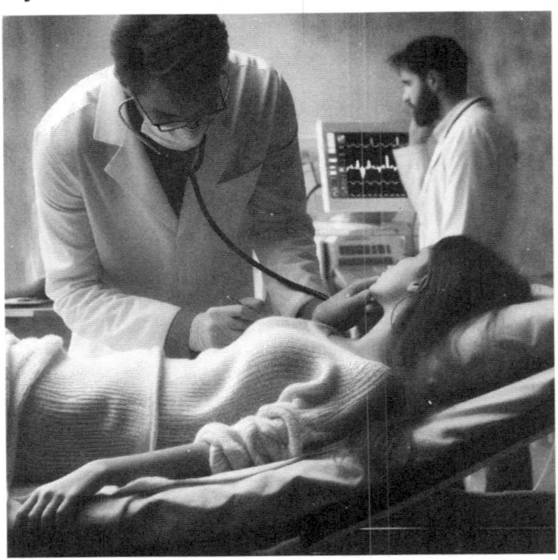

Samrat examining injured Shanaya

She wanted to talk but her eyes spoke more than her throat. She held my hand and said softly, "Hey doc! Thanks a lot." The same words that she said when we met for the first time. She smiled as she said so with a wincing tone. I shifted her to the ward room and told her to take some rest. I arranged for all her scans to be done. Thankfully, there were no fractures or fatal injuries. I called Constable Mr. *Yadav* so that he could inform her family. She gave her husband's number and the information was sent. Her husband was away for a while but I told *Shanaya* to assure him that his wife is safe and has not sustained any major injuries. He messaged that he would take a while to reach as he was in Aerocity *Gurgaon* which is approximately 35 kilometres from our hospital. I texted him not to worry and things will be fine. *Shanaya* also felt relieved.

The safety of our near and dear ones is all that is needed sometimes. Nothing in this world seems more important than assuring that your loved one is fine and safe. I was feeling the same relief after seeing *Shanaya* talking normally. I met her after a decade but she was still the same. The five feet two inches girl with a fair complexion, skinnier as before, an hour glass shape, V shaped face cut, rose petal lips and a mole on the right cheek. A perfect looking girl a guy would die for. I had no regrets in my life for whatever I had done so far in my life. The success and failures were all mine, were all my decisions but, I do regret for her sometimes. And I do wonder if I could rewind and change things my way for this chapter of my life. I sometimes feel helpless. I proposed but she disposed.

I asked *Shanaya,* if she would like a cup of tea. She said, she would if I accompany her. Although hard-pressed but I could not resist myself as I got an opportunity to relive those moments with a cup of tea. I sat by her bedside on a chair. The tea was served in paper cups with *matthis*. I handed her the cup of tea and one *matthi* as I knew she loved it that ways.

I held my cup in the right hand. I preferred the tea without *matthis*.

Shanaya asked me about my family. I told her that I was not married yet but not single either. I was in a relationship with *Chandani*, a pathologist in our hospital and had plans to get married soon. She did not ask me anything more about *Chandani*.

Shanaya told me that her husband *Victor Verma* ran a property dealing business in Noida and they had a two year old son named *Ayaan*.

I got out of my thoughts and tried to ask her about the accident. I wanted to discuss about many things with her, our dates, our past, our love and ourselves, but, the curiosity about the accidental outbreak masqueraded the romance inside me. Sometimes a true professional has to leave his love behind his duties. Although by convention a medico falls in love with his/her comedico student only but I unconventionally, fell in love with a non medico student a decade ago. I won't call myself out of the box but I perhaps found love in a different basket.

Shanaya told me that she works in a construction company as an architect in Noida. She had to leave for a seminar at 6:30 am from her home so she decided to drive by herself as her husband would leave only after 9 am. She took the *Sharda* bridge and was driving towards Noida. She played her favourite song at the top of its volume while she was driving. She said, "I was slightly overspeeding but there was no traffic so I preferred driving at my comfortable speed." There was nothing to be felt suspicious or scared of. It was around 6:45 by then, when she noticed a car moving across the road approximately ten metres ahead of her. She suddenly applied the brakes without slowing down which left her car skidding by around two hundred and seventy degrees leading to the collision with the divider. Her head impacted with the steering. While she was semiconscious with her eyes slightly drooping, she saw that the car which was crossing her was slowly disappearing in the midst of the smog. She fell unconscious on the steering wheel. She was brought to the hospital by the Police Control Room van. She next opened her eyes with me standing by her side.

I asked her about the other car which crossed her just before the accident. She said it was a sedan, indigo in colour, looked an expensive one but she was not sure about its brand. I asked her whether she could see its driver. She said she was not sure about it.

The pattern was almost the same. Early morning hours, the other vehicle disappearing like a flash of light, there was no trace of it before or after the accident.

I was now more curious to solve this mystery as now *Shanaya* had been a victim of it and had a close escape. Although I met her after a decade but I had the same concern and affection for her as it was before. There are a few things in life which never change. They are independent functions of time. In all these years, I never tried to contact her or tried to find out how she was. There was no connection on social media either. Her coincidental meeting in such a situation left a part of my brain numb and lost in flashback. I told *Shanaya* to take some rest and started her intravenous drip at the requisite rate.

Flashback-2

It was my first date and second meeting with *Shanaya*. I had already saved her number in the first meeting. I did not call her for the next two days as the feelings of meeting her were still sinking deep in my heart and I was trying to adapt to them. I called her the next weekend and perhaps she was waiting eagerly for my call.

We met at Ola Sizzlers in Connaught Place. *Shanaya* ordered a good *tandoori* sizzler with a mouth watering fragrance. As she picked up the piece of *paneer* and dipped it in mint *chutney*, she asked, "Why did you take so long to call me?" I admitted blushingly that I was late because I was preoccupied. She replied, "Busy doctor *sahab*." I gently shrugged my shoulders. We sipped the virgin mojito with extra lemon added and ice crushing with two straws dipped in one glass. As we sipped, we looked at each other with a smile, holding the straws with pursed lips. We quickly finished our lunch and rushed to the Odeon cinema to watch the block buster movie *Ashiqui* 2 starring *Aditya Roy Kapoor* playing *Rahul* and *Shraddha Kapoor* playing *Arohi*. The movie portrayed the life of a celebrity singer *Rahul* who got into alcohol and drug addictions. *Shanaya* started crying when she saw *Rahul* living a lifeless life. She felt extremely sympathetic for *Arohi* who persuaded *Rahul* to quit alcohol for her. *Shanaya* was sulking. Thanks to the song by *Arijit Singh, "Tum hi ho….."* with its

heart touching lyrics by *Mithoon*. As the song played we both got overwhelmed. Our hearts were pounding with audible beats against our chest wall. I held her right hand while she embraced me with the other and we got closer to each other. I took a deep breath and she slowly locked her lips with mine. As I gently sucked her rose petal lips my right hand rubbed her breast and I gently squeezed it. She spanked me for that squeeze and giggled gently while our lips were still locked till the song ended; it was the intermission and the lights were switched on. We immediately sat straight and I realised that I had spoiled her lipstick. She took out a tissue paper from her bag and cleaned her philtrum and chin.

We both looked at each other with extreme love and affection and utmost satisfaction. It appeared we needed no one but each other to be happy and lively. Just one word, just one person, just one soul that's *Shanaya,* who became the whole world for me in last few minutes. None of us blinked our eyes till the movie resumed. *Shanaya* held my hand tightly throughout the movie and was in tears when *Rahul* died at the end.

Samrat and Shanaya watching the movie

Addictions of any sort do not lead you to happy ending. It's always wiser to quit them just at the right time before it's too late. Fortunately, none of us was in those addictions. After watching the anguished demise of *Rahul* one cannot even think of getting into one.

Some More Clues.....

While I was walking through the corridor in my thoughts a voice startled me. He was our ward boy *Vikas Tiwari,* "Dr. sahab! When will you operate my sister for the fracture in her arm?"

"Don't worry *Tiwari,* we will do it by tomorrow for sure," I replied.

Yes sir, I understand, "There have been a large number of emergency cases so the elective ones take a back seat."

The patterns of the accidental outbreak were worth understanding. But surprisingly no one was taking it seriously. The media houses were blaming the traffic police and the traffic lights. The traffic police was blaming the municipality. The municipality was blaming the over speeding vehicles.

Deep inside my heart, I knew that something is terribly wrong over there and none of the government bodies need to be blamed. The *Sharda* bridge had one of the best roads in the city with automated traffic signals. None of the signals malfunctioned in the last couple of years. I was clueless.

Was it only my presumption that something is wrong?

Well, this could be an unfortunate coincident only?

Did the patterns I observe really exist or those were my imaginations?

If it were so consistent, why didn't the police officials think about it?

"Well *Tiwari,*" I asked, "How is that head injury boy now, who met with an accident a couple of days before? Did he manage to survive?"

"Sir, he is paralysed. He cannot feel or move his all four limbs. He does not have any urine or stool sensation. His life will be totally dependent now. He just has a mouth to eat and lungs to breathe. At such a young age he will be dependent instead of shouldering his family", replied *Tiwari.*

I decided to visit that boy in order to get some answers or atleast some clues for my questions. I reached the neurosurgery ward. The scene there was extremely breathtaking. The ward census had exceeded the maximum capacity by five folds. I searched for that boy on each bed and finally found him. I introduced myself and asked him about a brief narration of the event. He introduced himself to me as *Aryan* and said that he works in a software company in Noida and was going to his office the usual way through the *Sharda* bridge. He was over speeding as he was in a hurry but was not rash at all.

He saw a trailer crossing the road in front of his car. It was a huge trailer and would have been spotted from a distance if it was there before. As per the narration, given by *Aryan* the trailer was spotted only after it was at an unavoidable distance. He tried to avoid and took a sharp turn without getting a chance to slow down. The car turned three hundred and sixty degrees and his head banged against the car ceiling five times. "What was the direction of the trailer in which it was moving?", I asked. *Aryan* replied that it moved from left to right in front of his car. "Ok, so we can say that if your car was moving along the *x axis* the trailer was moving along the *y axis*, correct *Aryan*?" I asked.

"Well that's how you can put it doctor," replied *Aryan.*

Shanaya also gave a similar kind of description of the accident and she was also over speeding.

Over speeding and the vehicle's trajectory at right angles to each other were the two new clues that were added to my list.

I decided to get back to *Shanaya* to check the status of her recovery and gather some more information from her about the incident. I knocked at her door and pushed the door slightly to check if she is alright. She was resting quietly in her bed which was slightly propped up at the head end to give her more comfort. The lights were switched off but the rays of the setting sun illuminated the room bright enough for me to see her.

Her, special kind of cell phone, a kind of model that I had never seen before was lying on the side table . It was almost the same size as that of the normal smartphone but it was slightly thicker. It had a dial like knob on the top right corner and a halo of light was illuminating from its screen. I wanted to see that cell phone once. The loud announcement on the hospital system woke *Shanaya* up; she got up with a moan and saw me standing at the entrance of her ward room as she turned her head towards the door. She picked up her cell phone and kept it inside her bag before I could ask anything about it.

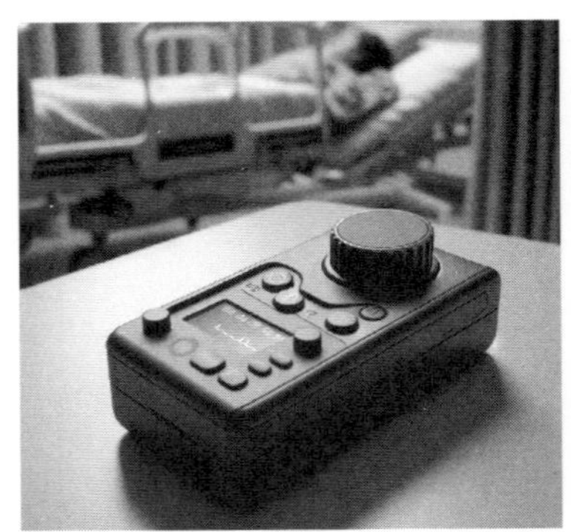

Shanaya's special kind of cellphone

She called me inside by waving her fingers and said that *Victor* (her husband) has sent a text that he would take some more time to reach as he is stuck in the traffic. I told her about over speeding and the perpendicular movement of the two vehicles. She ignored and said *Samrat*, "We have met after ten long years." She looked at me with that serene love in her eyes. I forgot everything for that moment. She reminded me of our date when we met near the *Kotla* cricket stadium not far from my medical college.

Flashback-3

It was late evening in the summer when I was returning from my clinical posting to the boy's hostel. We decided to meet in the backyard of the *Kotla* cricket stadium nearby my medical college. It was 7 pm and *Shanaya* was supposed to be home by thirty past eight, so we practically had very scarce time to spend. We decided to date in car itself. I bought a rose, a glass of hot chocolate fudge and a box of Ferrero Rocher (her favourite). I picked her up from the nearby metro station and we drove to the stadium and parked the car along the pavement in the backyard of the stadium. There were no cricket matches going on in that season. So practically, the stadium and its vicinity were left abandoned. It had already started raining as it was last week of June, the usual time of arrival of monsoon in Delhi.

I offered her the rose and gently uncovered the glass of hot chocolate fudge with my car keys and dropped two spoons into it so that we could have it together. *Shanaya* picked up a Rocher and clenched gently between her teeth with part of it outside her lips which she offered to me. I slowly bowed closer to her lips, licked the sweet chocolate ball and then her juicy lips. The hot chocolate got spilled all over the dashboard. I reclined her car seat then gently untucked her shirt and then rubbed her lower back to relieve her everlasting backache which she suffered from because of her

exhaustive dance practice sessions. She said sarcastically, "So doc, are you making love or treating me for my backache?" I replied mischievously, "Well, dear madam! You have a dual advantage today."

Samrat and Shanaya inside the car

She laid with her eyes closed. The white noise of rain and the sweet petrichor made the car's ambience no less than a honeymoon suite. She unbuttoned my shirt and we snogged for a while. I crushed the Rochers on her breasts and sucked those chocolaty nipples passionately. We intended to take it to the climax but left it for the next date. I helped her dressing herself again something which we guys never intend to do. A girl not just deserves your love but also the respect. A thorough gentleman must be able to offer both of them to her lady, because love without respect seems just like a basic instinct. I quickly dropped her at a safe distance from her home in *Greater Kailash* that day. I started my car once I made sure that she had entered her apartment.

The Shockingly Shocking Meet

While we both recalled that date, she looked at me with a charming lovely look, blushing a bit and we both took a deep breath and rubbed our watering eyes.

I asked her to recall if car's trajectory was at right angle to her. She said, yes it was that ways only.

Now I could slowly correlate what happened with me the last Friday. A truck blew me out of my mind when I was sloping down the *Sharda* bridge. I was wondering why I could not see it in my rear view mirror. I could now understand that it must have appeared and vanished perpendicular to my car.

"Why are you so inquisitive about the mode of accident doc?" asked *Shanaya*.

"That is because it made us meet after a decade, so I was wondering how it could take place repeatedly so that we can meet again and again." I replied facetiously.

After looking at *Shanaya*'s reaction I realized that I cracked a bad joke with absolutely wrong timing.

She said, "I don't have to meet with an accident to meet you doc. I can meet you otherwise as well. So please improve your sense of humour for the next time. "

I was about to wind up the day's work to go back home. I saw an old looking man wearing loose white shirt, traditional pleated pant with sports shoes, golden chain watch (certainly not gold) and had a slight paunch. He had a dark complexion.

He introduced himself as *Victor's* driver. He said, "I am *Victor* Sir's driver. I am here to pick up *Shanaya* mam. I told him that we need to observe her for the next twenty four hours to monitor her vitals; so he could get her discharged the next day. "Does someone from the family need to stay with madam for tonight?" the driver asked. I told him that there is no obvious need but if they wished one of them could stay.

At least *Victor* should have come to see *Shanaya* but it seems he is too busy for this. Well I had no business to judge him but I was expecting *Shanaya*'s husband to visit her while she was admitted.

I took my evening ward round and decided to leave for home. I was scared but it was not getting on to my nerves. I had to be safe. So I thought let's unfollow the patterns that I observed. I decided to leave till the sunset was complete so that I could avoid the twilight time. I drove my car with an average speed even though it was a clear stretch of the road. While I was sloping down I saw a woman crossing the road with a pram, carrying a baby in it. I applied brakes to avoid any injury to them and I was able to execute it well because my car was within speed limits. Both the pram and the lady disappeared as soon as I applied the brakes. I drove back home slowly.

Fortunately, I did not suffer any injury. I gained some confidence that I could travel across the *Sharda* bridge safely. That pram and the lady were not getting off my mind though.

I parked my car and started walking towards my home. The street looked a bit gloomy today perhaps because the streetlights malfunctioned. I knocked at the door. A beautiful white girl with blonde hair stepped out of my house and asked me who I was. I was shaken. What kind of joke this was. I pinched myself to see if I was alive and not dreaming. The lady asked whom did I want to meet.

"My mother, my sister, my brother, my sister in-law and my dearly loved niece." I replied in a soft but affirmative tone.

She said, "Sir, I am *Barbara Brown* residing with my family in this house for almost two decades ever since I got married. I neither saw you here nor did I hear the names of your dear ones you rattled just now." She left me totally confused.

I did not take alcohol, I was not drunk, I haven't taken any substance of abuse ever since I watched *Ashiqui* 2.

"Madam, am I standing at 296 *Taj Apartments Pitampura*"? I asked.

Samrat turning back to his car after unexpectedly meeting Barbara Brown

She said, No, this is 114, Henfield drive, Solihull, England. I missed a few heartbeats, turned back and walked a few steps towards my car. I immediately took out my cell phone to call *Chandani*.

"Why don't you come inside? You are already late today and you are going towards your car again? What's wrong with you? Come inside and have dinner. You haven't even answered my calls," said a familiar voice in a yelling tone. I was already confused, startled, bewildered and could not trust my very existence in this world. I stopped again, turned back towards supposedly my house or someone else's house perhaps. I saw my mother standing at the porch with her face flushed red in anger. I got such a relief that her anger was not enough to bother me. I walked again towards my house. I touched my face, head and neck etc to make sure that I was not in any kind of an illusion. My mother felt it so weird when I was touching myself and she said, "It's 2 am, where have you been all this time. Wait, firstly you were not sure about your house, you were walking back towards your car, then you touched yourself and you are quite late. Did you go to the pub with *Karan* and *Rajendra*?" asked Mumma in a rapid fire questionnaire. I did not say anything for a while but then just to calm her down, I said I was stuck in an emergency surgery at the Hospital.

2 am, how was that possible? I started by 7:30 pm from the city hospital after the sunset and should have been home by eight. I did not stop anywhere. There was no traffic. I found almost all signals turned green. The way from city hospital to my home is roughly forty minutes by car.

So, I was approximately six hours delayed and was completely clueless about what happened with me during that time. I encountered a blonde lady in Henfield drive in Solihull, England. I checked my wallet, my watch, my gold chain and my cell phone. I just wanted to make sure that I have not been a victim of some antisocial element. The locality around the city hospital is full of drug addicts and pickpockets. Well, fortunately, everything was in place.

Oh dear God! If you really exist then please make me believe what I have just gone through because all this seems unbelievable to me. I could not sleep that night. My mother slept in her own room. I had no one to discuss the incident with as it was too late. Even if I do discuss it with someone, who would have believed me? Deep inside my heart I knew that it was certainly not an illusion or delusion but the truth.

Eureka!

The next day I found it hard to get up because I could hardly take a sound sleep. I managed to get ready on time, had a quick bite with freshly prepared orange juice and stepped out of my house to reach the car parked at a few metres from my home. There was another surprise waiting for me. My car was soiled with mud, the tyres looked muddy. As far as I could recall there was not a single drop falling from the skies, the clouds were out of question and the roadway from city hospital to my home had no muddy patch at all. It was a clean, smooth and newly constructed road. I was getting late so I ignored it and drove to the hospital for the day's work.

I was quite happy as I had to meet *Shanaya* today on rounds. My excitement for round was slightly more than a fresh post graduate medical student that day. I met *Shanaya* on round; I greeted her a bit formally as I was with my team of doctors to which she reacted with a snigger but romantic look. I told her that she will be discharged by the evening of that day. I could not see *Victor*, perhaps because he had already left for his office by then. I had the elective operation theatre day that day. I told *Shanaya* softly when my team was on the next bed for round visit that I will have coffee with her after the operation theatre work and then discharge her. So that, she can inform the driver to reach by 6 pm or so. I finished the OT list by 3 pm. After 5 hours of exhaustive work when you have not had a good night sleep what all you need is a cup of coffee. I went quietly but swiftly to *Shanaya*'s ward room to have a cup of coffee with her. Perhaps she was also eagerly waiting because her eyes were focused right at the doorway when I entered her room. As soon as she saw me at the entrance she pretended looking the other way. Well I knew this habit of hers from good old times. Habits die hard but there are a certain habits of your loved ones which you never want them to get away with because they make you fall in love with them again and again.

I sat next to her and the coffee that I had ordered arrived. I handed over her cup like a gentleman. *Shanaya* asked about my red looking eyes. I thought I could share my incident with her without any hesitation because I was sure that she won't judge me for anything and would surely believe in what I say. I narrated *Shanaya* what had happened with me last night. *Shanaya* listened to me carefully while she sipped her coffee and surprisingly she was not surprised. I asked, "Are you not surprised?" She said, not at all. She said, **what happened to you is nothing but a travel to another dimension.** She asked how I could be surprised with it. I said anybody would. "*Samrat,* don't you remember what you told me when we talked the very last time?" *Shanaya* asked.

I was stunned and speechless as I remembered.

Flashback-4

That was our last date and we never thought that it would be our last one. We went to *Saket Select City Walk*. It was a hot sunny afternoon. We sat down in one of the auditoriums of the multiplex cinema to watch the fourth movie of the famous Harry Potter series. Who in the end went for a movie! As soon as the lights turned off, we got started. This time *Shanaya* was more passionate for me. She kissed every single centimetre of my lips, face, forehead, and neck, licked my ears and hugged me so tightly as if I was going away from her. She then sulked and burst into tears. We decided to quit the movie and I took her out to talk . We sat down in the cafeteria of the mall. She disclosed that her family members were forcing her to seek matches. So it was high time that I take some decision. Well, though I had just finished MBBS at that time but I was waiting for my post graduate entrance exam; for which I had prepared over the last six months of my internship. I always wanted to secure a top rank but our NEET PG exam was postponed on the eve of the scheduled date. The exam board gave a pretext of some security reasons for not conducting the exam on the scheduled date. The fresh date of the exam was not disclosed and was unlikely to be declared until recently at that time.

We, the medico students had protested, wrote letters to the PMO for the new date and marched to the parliament but none of competent authorities focused on this issue as it was

a minor problem for them. I always knew that I had to get married to *Shanaya* but what am I going to feed her without a financial security. I told her to wait and let the things settle down until I decide my medical branch of specialization. She did not say anything further. Perhaps her silence was a warning for me which I could not perceive. We did not get back to watch the movie. We had a quick lunch and then I dropped her. She hugged me with clenched fingers on my shoulder and embraced me as close to her breast as she could. It felt something but everything very normal except that it appeared more intense.

She did not call or message me for one week. I tried calling her but she did not answer. I dropped messages but she did not reply. The exam got rescheduled and was supposed to take place in next one week. I tried every single mean to get in touch with *Shanaya* but she was not responding. I got occupied with the preparations and after an exhaustively brainstorming test I could secure a good rank to get my dream branch of specialization. I wanted to share it with *Shanaya* if she could just receive my call. She did not.

Three weeks passed. It was first time in our divine relationship of last three years that we did not talk to each other for this long. The next day all was set for the counselling. I had made all preparations with my documents and scorecard. Finally, I opted for Masters in Orthopaedics at All India College of Medical Sciences (AICMS). I was so happy that I called *Shanaya* even before anyone in my family. She did not answer. I dropped a message regarding the result, 'Got MS orthopaedics in AICMS just now.'

She replied, 'Congratulations! Got engaged to Mr. *Victor*, just now.'

I did not know what to reply I could not even congratulate her. I did not know whether to celebrate or to moan. The cosmos gave me from one hand and took away from the other. I called her and she finally answered my call. I congratulated her. She was sulking. I told her to break up with *Victor* immediately as it was only a small *ROKA* ceremony but she said that her mother would have another heart attack if she does so. Her mother already had one. Her brother's marriage was awaited because of her own marriage and finally *Victor*'s mother is the best friend of *Shanaya's* mother. I tried to persuade her that neither her parents nor her brother would live her life. She had to live her life on her own. She failed to listen or understand perhaps because her fear of going against her family was greater than her love for me at that moment. I told her that the cosmos can never give you anything unless you strive for it. It's not very late, we can still make up but there seemed no hopes. If you want to win any battle of life then you have to conquer your fear first. Both of us had our own fears. I had it before I could enter into my specialization and she had it after she was *ROKAFIED*.

I hung up after saying my last words to her, "It's ok if we cannot meet in this dimension but if we love each other truly and to the core then some other dimension will make us reunite in some other space-time". I decided that day that I would never talk to her. I blocked all the communication channels from social media as well. I deleted her number from my phonebook but could not delete it from my mind book. I always remembered it by heart.

The Definitive Clue

I remembered what I had said to her. Those thoughts came to me from my deep seated belief in quantum world and cosmos. But, I was startled how *Shanaya* could remember those words so correctly. I said those lines to her so as to end our conversation on a positive note. I asked *Shanaya* how did she remember everything so correctly. "I remember every single word that you said to me doc," said *Shanaya*. I never thought that we will meet again on any fine day but, your last words always gave me some hope that someday we will meet again and reconcile our relationship. I was shaken to the core.

The question that was seeking an answer about the accidental epidemic seems to find a definitive clue now. The *Sharda* bridge has become a zone of multidimensional commutation which has been leading to the accidents and the shocking event that happened with me last night.

I prepared *Shanaya*'s discharge and told the receptionist to inform *Shanaya's* driver so that he could pick up *Shanaya* on time. I asked *Shanaya* how was she so sure that whatever happened with me last night is another dimension travel. She said, "I don't know what happened with you exactly but I have always trusted your words like the voice of the cosmos because I loved you from my soul, hence when I met you again, I could only conclude that our meeting was an authentication of your last words that you said to me. I always believed that whatever open ways to new dimension will make you meet me again. Thank you Doc! I take your leave."

She departed but left a clue to solve my problem.

Karan was one such person in our medical college who was as interested in this phenomenon of nature and the belief of multi dimension. So I decided to discuss the phenomenon with him and *Rajendra* as no one else seemed interested to go to the core of this accidental epidemic. I took both of them to the café and discussed the matter with them. *Rajendra* was clueless as to what I was discussing about. *Karan* of course had some idea. I also shared with them what happened to me last night.

"Please elaborate", said *Rajendra*.

The Multidimensions Explained to *Rajendra*

I began, "So *Raju* (*Rajendra*'s nickname) we live in a three dimensional or 3D world where we can travel forward-backward, left-right or up-down and all these dimensions can be put as length, breadth and height. Now all these dimensions remain in synchronization with time which can be regarded as the fourth dimension." One can move in either direction *i.e.* back and forth in all three dimensions but the time is a dimension that always moves forward. It can be understood by the fact that we have only grown older in age from infant to toddler, to child to teenager, to youth to the current age. We can understand this by an analogy.

See that small but long furrow alongside the wall. It appears one dimensional for us *Raju* because we see it as a line. Now, imagine a small mouse, crawling in that furrow (Fig-16.1), while going through its journey through that furrow it moves on both its walls to and fro, sometimes its floor and comes out through the other end. For that mouse, the furrow is three dimensional. One can now easily imagine that we three are like that mouse sitting in this café which is a like a furrow for someone who is looking at this cafe from a distance. That will be called as the fifth dimension. This way you can very well visualize that every next dimension has a higher one looked upon to itself from a distance that will eventually lead us into the outer space for the last dimension. One thing is common for all these dimensions that they all are connected to each other through time. Like for that mouse and us, time will be the same even though we are at a higher dimension from him.

Fig-16.1 (a mouse crawling in a furrow, viz a 3-D space for the mouse but it is a single line in one dimension for someone seeing it from a distance)

The dimensions if plotted on a piece of paper as parallel lines (Fig-16.2) which will get connected with each other through time lines at different instants. So they will form a space time grid, a well explained concept in the quantum physics. *Raju* said that he has understood it to quite some extent but how does this explain the accidental epidemic on *Sharda* bridge.

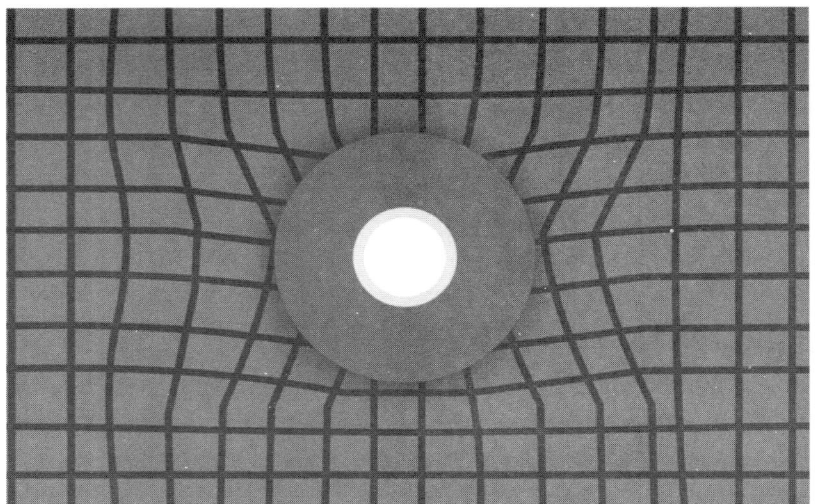

*Fig-16.2 (a **Space-time Grid**[1], in which the points of intersection of parallel lines represent different Time Instants, the parallel lines distort when a celestial object with heavy mass disturbs the evenness of this grid, owing to its heaviness)*

Well this is just the background I added. The real concept is yet to come.

The Real Concept

Raju said that he cannot wait long to understand it further as he was finding it quite interesting. So now, there is fair idea that we have got about the space time grid.

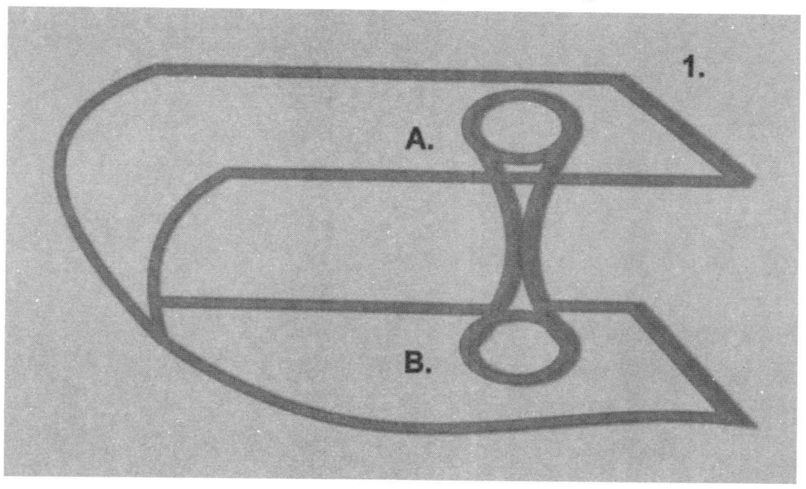

Fig-17.1 (two points A and B at a shortest distance to each other)

Imagine two points at a distance on this piece of paper (considering it a space time grid) point A and point B. If we were to find the shortest distance between the two points to join them then how that could be done. As expected, *Raju* drew a straight line to join the two points. *Karan* now intervened and said, let's fold this paper like this (Fig-17.1). Now the two points are at a shortest distance to each other and the path which will make us reach from point A to point B in this folded space time grid is called as the **WORMHOLE**[2]. Now you see that this wormhole can make one travel from one dimension to another with a considerably shortest distance.

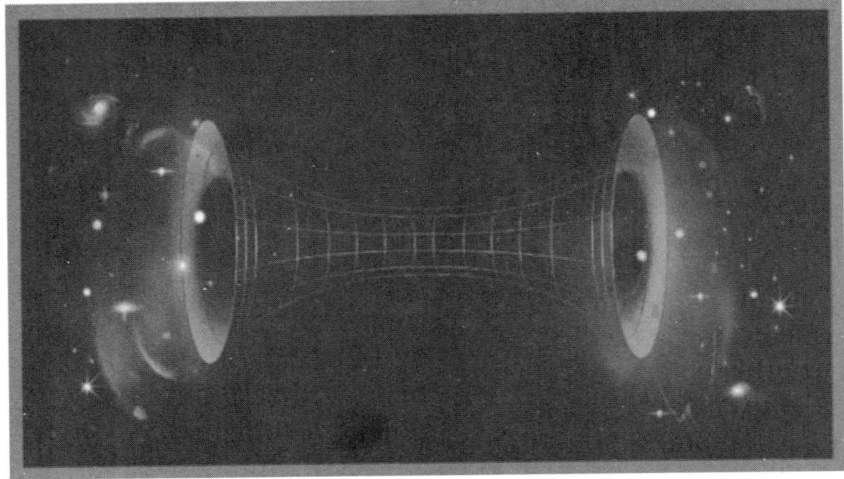

Fig-17.2 (a hypothetical structure of a Wormhole)

"Ok friends, but where do these wormholes exist and why we can't see them if they really exist?" asked *Raju*.

The Wormhole

One cannot see them because they are too small to be seen, billionth size of a centimetre. For their existence, they exist everywhere. Just like when we travel on the road, it appears to be an evenly constructed corridor but there is lot of unevenness on its surface consisting of small cracks and crevices; which one can only appreciate if one observes them as closely as possible. So, no surface is as smooth as it appears to be. They are full of irregularities. The space time grid is no exception to it. The space time grid is also full of irregularities in it which makes it susceptible to the existence of wormholes. "So, now how does this explain the *Sharda* bridge mystery?"

"We cannot jump to conclusions, *Raju,*" I said.

We now had the background knowledge which has led us to the same page. What is the most probable hypothesis is that some disorderliness is leading to the wormholes being opened at the *Sharda* Bridge. The exact cause of the same can be deduced by self experience only. "What do you mean?" asked both *Karan* and *Raju,* simultaneously. "I mean what I said," I replied. We all looked at each other in surprise and some fear. After a silence, *Karan* said that it was already late evening and as per the pattern it may take place either at dawn or dusk. "So let's plan for tomorrow morning," said *Rajendra.*

Both *Karan* and *Raju* were scared to go to the core of the problem. *Karan* said that no one is worried about it then why should we. It was not our job I knew but as a doctor my job was not just to treat the disease but also prevent it. This epidemic has no vaccination unlike Covid but if we get to the core of the problem we can actually prevent this just like a vaccine prevents diseases.

The Night Before Self Experience

Karan said well, "We are definitely going to visit tomorrow but *Samrat* sir you have already experienced something last night." I remembered what he was talking about. *Karan* told me to check my GPS history so that I could actually make out where all did I travel. Did I really go to the Henfield drive in the United Kingdom or it was some kind of an illusion.Well, that was a simple but a brilliant idea given by *Karan*. That's the reason why they usually say that common sense is quite uncommon. I opened my GPS history and found something which blew us out of our minds. The trajectory of the path travelled showed that I had travelled to the United Kingdom but the distance travelled was less than one kilometre. What it signified was that I travelled to the UK but perhaps through the shortest distance that anyone had travelled so far. *Karan*'s idea to check the GPS history was simple but meticulous common sense. It does explain that I travelled to another country and back to my own with a few hundred metres pathway; perhaps through a wormhole that connected the *Sharda* Bridge and a place in the other part of the world in some other time.

The other aspect of the incident that the time elapsed was 6 hours more than the expected time.

I had supposedly spent not more than five minutes talking to that blonde lady named *Barbara Brown* and then I turned back towards my car until my mother called me from the back.

It was now *Raju's* turn as he had a lucid idea of what we were explaining to him.

He said, see guys if the space-time grid distorts to join two distant points, point A and point B through a wormhole then the time curves also bend. Since the time curve shows a bend, it is obvious that time elapsed between two points will not be the same. It is not very difficult to understand. If the space-time grid is deforming then time will deform too, according to the configuration of the wormhole. I was really delighted that *Raju* also understood this phenomenon. It appeared that time dilated during my experience of last night. *The few minutes of my time in the other dimension was equivalent to few hours of my time in present dimension*. This is called as '**Time Dilation**[3]' (Fig-19.1). Clocks in airplanes click at different rates as compared to clocks on the ground. If we put a clock on a high mountain keeping it stationary, it results in slightly different rates compared to a clock based on the ground.

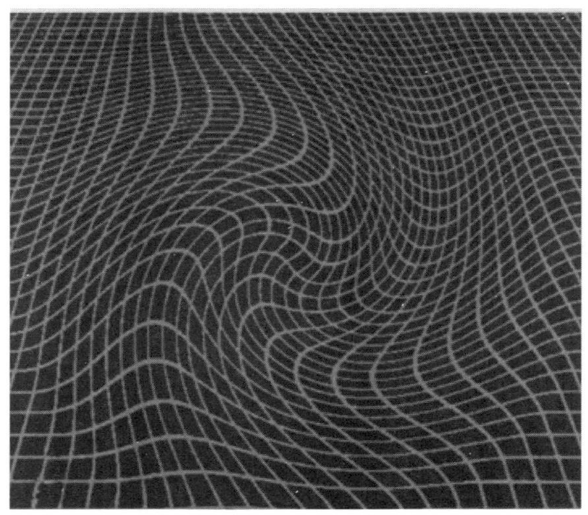

Fig-19.1 A distorted space-time grid that impacts the elapsed time through time dilation

The Early Morning Visit to *Sharda* Bridge

All three of us *i.e.* I, *Karan* and *Raju* reached the *Sharda* bridge at 4 am sharp when it was all dark and still two hours to sunrise. The street dogs were barking as if we had disturbed their privacy. We parked by the roadside on the top of the bridge with parking lights on. We waited quietly for the next one and half hour but nothing happened. We got off the car and looked here and there. The sky was slowly turning red at the horizon of the river *Yamuna*. We never knew that our city could look this mesmerizing at any point of the day. We always knew Delhi as a polluted city with full of hassles.

We looked at the river from the top. Something unusual drew our attention on the bridge. We saw a kind of smoldering ring in the smog around ten metres ahead of our car. Nothing had happened so far on the bridge, so all three of us decided to go closer to this unusual phenomenon. As soon as we got off the car we could not gather the strength to go closer to it. We asked a beggar, lying down on the sidewalk taking his weedpuff, about the smoldering ring. He said that he has been seeing this for the last few weeks. It appears during the dawn and the dusk and disappears by itself. He said he had never seen such a thing before in last three decades of his life ever since he had been living on that sidewalk. It is just in the

last few weeks that he had been noticing this. I asked him, did he not try to find out what it was. He said, "I have my own work to do and have to earn daily bread for my family. I earn my living by digging the sand on the bank of the *Yamuna* river that flows under the bridge apart from begging. This smoldering thing never created a problem in my life so I did not care for it. As it will disappear in sometime on its own."

Samrat, Rajendra and Karan visiting Sharda bridge in early morning

While we were only trying to figure out the cause of smoldering ring we heard a loud bang behind us at a distance of around 20 metres from us. *Raju* said, "I think we missed it." *Karan* said, "I always said not to bother about that smoldering ring. Now see, we missed it." I listened to both of them while all three of us were standing next to the beggar, and turned back immediately. We could hear the loud noise of the collision. We rushed towards the site. It took us five minutes to get there as it was a foggy day and the visibility was poor. It was a European model car. We went closer to the car to see if the driver and passengers were alright. I was bewildered to see the lady sitting on the driving seat. She was *Barbara Brown* whom I met a day before perhaps in my illusion.

She was moaning and semiconscious, asking for help from us. I told *Karan* and *Raju* that she is the same lady that I was talking about. They both thought I am hallucinating. They gave me a ridiculous look. I told *Karan* to take her to the private nursing home of his father so that we can at least ask her about what she saw. *Karan* asked, "Why not in a Government City Hospital?" I replied, "See man, she is not a normal patient. She must have definitely come from the dimension in which I got lost. So, she has to be treated that ways. You have all good facilities in your nursing home. We can treat her well and then she may unleash some of our concerns. I think we are about to get to the depth of this problem through her."

All three of us took her to the hospital run by *Karan*'s father. The treatment was immediately started. *Karan*'s father assured us that he will take a good care of her.

We left for our work at the city hospital and decided to return by evening.

That day it was more hectic than the usual days. There were six accidental cases brought to the hospital ER from the *Sharda* bridge. One of the patients among the accident victims was a young girl in her adolescence. She could hardly breathe. She was gasping for her last breath. She drew our attention immediately and we triaged her on utmost priority. Code blue was declared in the hospital. The entire team rushed to resuscitate her. We took all life supporting measures but she ultimately succumbed to death. Every single death was breaking us from inside. *Raju* was completely grieved by her death. He said that we had to ascertain the cause of this accidental epidemic and take measures to stop it with immediate effect. It was not a good beginning of the day to see a young girl losing her life like a house of cards crashing in fractions of seconds. We finished our work. It was *Karan*'s

Operation theatre day that day. He was stuck in a complex fracture fixation. So, we decided to wait for him with a cup of tea. *Raju* said, "What do you think? Are you sure that the lady whom we have left at *Karan's* hospital is the same *Barbara Brown* that you met in some kind of an illusion."

"First and foremost, how can you say that it was my illusion? We all saw the GPS history of my Google maps. Secondly, even if I am not sure but we have all the reasons to visit her, to get to the depth of the mystery. I am sure she can lead us somewhere,"I replied.

As soon as *Karan* was out of the OT we drove to his hospital. The lady was conscious by then and appeared in a reasonably good condition. *Karan*'s father had taken a good care of her. I went inside her room to see her. I thought if she is the same lady whom I met in my so called illusion by everyone, she would definitely recognize me. She looked at me, took a pause, hesitated a bit, swayed her head left and then to her right and asked, "Have we met before gentleman?"

"Perhaps yes or I guess no," I replied.

She introduced herself as *Barbara Brown*. She said that she lives in Solihull, United Kingdom with her husband and children. I looked at *Karan* and *Raju* with some victory and hopes. *Raju* looked the other way and asked, "So, what are you doing here madam?"

She said, she came to India to attend a condolence meeting of her very close Indian friend who passed away with her family two weeks back in a car accident. *Barbara* said that she was driving to her friend's home to attend her condolence meeting but unfortunately met with an accident. She rented a European model car for self driving as she wanted to explore the capital city as well. She said that her friend died with desires that left unfulfilled. She died with dreams which could never be realized.

I interrupted her impatiently, "We have all our condolences with your friend madam, may her soul rest in peace. We will really be grateful if you could just tell us what happened with you today morning just before the accident."

She looked at me with queer look and begun, "I was driving normally and certainly I was driving within the speed limits. I saw a big hole kind of a thing which tried to collapse in itself but something was forcefully holding it from collapsing. Some force was forcefully trying to keep that big large hole patent and prevented from collapsing. I saw a fast moving car coming from that hole and crossing my car. I was clueless and applied the brakes without slowing down and ended up colliding with the divider. My head banged against the steering wheel and I had a concussion. When I regained some consciousness I saw the three of you standing next to me. "

It was something abnormal for certain on the *Sharda* bridge that was taking place.Whether it was paranormal or had some scientific explanation. The mystery seemed difficult to solve but definitely not impossible now. There seemed a momentary opening of the entrance to the other dimension on the *Sharda* bridge which was the **Etiology**[4] behind the accidental epidemic. We still did not know why and how such a phenomenon was occurring at that place. What was so peculiar about this place?

All three of us, myself, *Raju* and *Karan* decided to do some research on the geography of this *Sharda* Bridge. I thought of involving my geologist friend, *Manoj*, from my school days.

The Expert Opinion

Manoj had studied geology from the University of Colorado. He had also worked on quantum physics projects in the Bell Labs of the USA. He was on a vacation to India due to the thanksgiving holidays in the USA that winters.

I called him up for a cup of coffee to *Karan*'s Hospital. He agreed and came on a single phone call. We both met each other after almost 8 long years and had lot of life to be discussed but, unfortunately I was eager to share our concerns with him to seek his help. We told him what all we had been going through in last few days.

Manoj thought for a while and said, "This is not paranormal but should have a scientific explanation."

"But then why this place only?", asked *Raju* and *Karan*.

"Only a significantly powerful disbalance in nature or a massive object can create such a level of disorderliness to give way to the opening of a wormhole. We should know the vicinity around the bridge inside out to ascertain the cause. Only the presence of an EXOTIC MATTER can open a worm hole." said *Manoj*.

"Exotic Matter?" I asked.

"An exotic matter is one that is said to have a **Negative Mass**[5] or you can say negative weight." said *Manoj*.

Looking all three of us puzzled he explained just as when we lift a dumbbell of say, weighing 5 kilograms it has a mass

of 5 kgs. If we happen to drop it, it will fall down immediately and perhaps on our toes. Now if this dumbbell would have been an exotic matter then its mass would be minus 5 kgs and in that case it will move in a direction opposite to the earth's gravitational pull. That means instead of falling on my toes it may go upwards like a *Diwali* cracker rocket and perhaps hit against the ceiling of this very room.

"Alright *Manoj*, but then why at *Sharda* bridge" I asked.

There is definitely something taking place which was creating an ambiguity in the natural existence of that place. An ambiguity here means disorderliness in the forces of nature.

"Recall everything from that morning of *Barbara Brown's* accident. The devil always resides in the detail." said *Manoj*.

So, we went, waited outside the car then suddenly the accidental thud blew all three of us. Wait, there was something that was missing between this, THE BEGGAR. The beggar told us that he earns his living by digging sand on the river bank.

"How can one earn his living by digging sand on the bank of the river?" asked *Manoj*.

"Let's go and find out."

Samrat, Rajendra, Karan and Manoj discussing with the beggar about the strange phenomenon

We reached the bridge with immediate effect and talked to that beggar. He told us that until last few weeks he was not able to earn well by begging but a big company guy came and hired all the beggars and fishermen to collect the sand from the bank of the *Yamuna* river and get it loaded in the trucks of the company. The work used to begin at 4 am and continued till sunrise when the commutation begins. The company was paying good wages to all of them. *Manoj* took a sample of this sand from that beggar after exhaustive efforts to coax him.

Manoj said that he would be testing this sand in his friend's private lab to get to the depth of the problem. The results were expected in the next 24 hours.

We had no alternative but to wait till the reports arrive. While I was driving back home I was thinking about *Shanaya*. The cosmos was kind enough to give me this opportunity to help in her tough time. I had a lot to share and to be shared but at least I was tranquilised that an incomplete chapter of my life touched a milestone by undusting the haze of time. I never knew that the words I told her in our last conversation before we parted would actually transpire. If I could have had another cup of coffee with her. The coffee was truly a coupling between us. Whenever we used to go out for movies she would actually sip my coffee with our lips locked. This gesture was like a soulful transference for both of us. We often read that love stories commence with coffee and terminates into wine; but for us coffee was the most divine aroma that had fragranced our relationship more than anything else in this universe.

Certain events in life change you forever. Love is an impetus to realise your dreams and it empowers you to do the unprecedented. *Shanaya*'s presence guided my pathway to solve the mystery of the accidental epidemic. Had *Shanaya* not reminded me of our last conversation, I would have never found the way ahead. I was eagerly waiting to hear about the laboratory results from *Manoj*. As a doctor I have always been interested in clinical laboratory reports of the patients but this time it was for the patients and not of the patients.

The Lab Reports

The next morning *Manoj* called us to meet him at the *Sharda* bridge. As it was a bank holiday we all reached to the bridge to meet him. He looked victorious but worried.

"So, let's start *Manoj*." I said very impatiently.

He said that the sand collected from the river bank contained **Superfluid**[6] Helium. The Helium gas, as we all know is used to fill in the air balloons. This helium converts into liquid when it is cooled to 3.2 degrees above **Absolute Zero**[7] temperature. Cooled down further it becomes a superfluid which is capable of flowing without resistance. In other words Superfluid Helium starts behaving as an exotic matter with a negative mass and flows against the direction of gravity *i.e.* upwards. The temperature around the river bank gets low to an extent that it gets the helium in the soil to become superfluid helium. This phenomenon occurs before the sunrise and after the sunset because the chilling winters and the smog add to the fall in temperature.

The superfluid helium so formed free flows against gravity and consequently on the *Sharda* bridge. It forms free flowing circles, as circle is the most stable shape for any free flowing fluid. As you must have seen that whenever it rains, the water falls from the skies in the form of tiny spherical droplets and not in the form of a splash. Now since these circles never collapse until the temperature changes they form

a suitable gateway to wormholes in the space-time. They open randomly in any space-time and allow trespassing of moving objects like cars, trucks and sometimes prams, as *Samrat* saw in one of his trips through the bridge, to our dimension and vice versa. So this explains it all, concluded *Manoj*.

Superfluid helium climbing up the bridge against the gravity

"But then if the wormholes are of billionth size of a centimetre then how do they allow the trespassing of such large sized objects?" *Karan* asked *Manoj*.

Manoj explained that he agrees that the original size of the wormhole is too small to allow the trespassing of any object and that's exactly the reason why we don't see the wormholes around us all the time. The wormhole collapses within itself due to its small size under the influence of gravity just like gas bubbles keep forming and deforming in a glass of any aerated drink say beer.

A balloon when inflated can grow to 10 times of its original volume but its mouth has to be tied in order to maintain it inflated else it will collapse. The same balloon can rise in the air against gravity if inflated with helium gas. In this case whatever is being filled inside the balloon is acting as an exotic matter exerting a continuously expanding force against the natural tendency of a balloon to deflate.

That's exactly what the exotic matter Superfluid Helium is doing in this case. It is expanding the wormhole against the natural gravity, just like an inflated balloon, large enough to accommodate big objects like cars and keeping it patent for a time long enough to allow trespassing.

We were all stunned by the flawless looking explanation given by *Manoj*.

"But why are the beggars paid so well for sand collection from the bank?", I asked.

Manoj said that the Superfluid Helium is a very good superconductor so they must be using it for semiconductor devices, which must be a tech company for whom the beggars were working.

Were they responsible in any form for the peculiar epidemic happening out there?

Manoj said that the digging of sand on the bank could have lead to the augmentation of the effect of the superfluid helium but we cannot hold them responsible for it as the reserves were there already. What they have been doing might be illegal but perhaps the company guys were unaware of the consequences themselves.

The Solution

Now that we had the cause of the accidental epidemic and a valid scientific explanation, the question now remains that how are we going to bring it to an end? The cause of the phenomenon was the extremely low temperature during the dawn and the dusk near the river bank as the surface of the water is exceptionally cold during these times of the day. We have all studied science as students of class ten and have knowledge that sodium when thrown in water has a rigorous inflammable reaction with water. If we could just spread sodium along the bank of the river running under the bridge we could just evade the phenomenon.

For how long and how many days that could have been done? We cannot do it every day.

Sodium reacting chemically with water

Manoj explained that this phenomenon is like a chain reaction. It has begun once and now being continued. The unconventional opening of a wormhole creates a bend in the space-time grid of that place. This bend is repaired by itself if only this vicious cycle is broken. If we stop it once to a halt at the time of its occurrence the other dimensional wormholes would no longer be opened. The only prerequisite was our timing had to be precise.

We decided to take the help of the beggars themselves. We called their leader and had a meeting with him. I told him, "You all have been seeing the anguished mishappenings around you almost everyday. I know it doesn't bother you and perhaps has no concern with your personal life but every life lost for no reason is a responsibility of the society. An unnatural death is a wakeup call for every civilization to come together and save the mankind. It tells us that something is not right with the atmosphere around us and we are in a state of imbalance with our mother nature. If not today then tomorrow it may take our lives as well, as death does not differentiate between the rich and the poor."

The team of beggars agreed with us after they realised our persuasion was totally selfless and had no personal gain. We made a plan.

When the beggars would go for sand collection the next morning we will give them bags of sodium crumbs for sprinkling near the river bank. They would sprinkle it along the entire length of the bank which runs under the bridge. We had planned to arrange sodium crumbs from my uncle Mr. *Jagdish,* who is a chemical merchant. *Manoj* did all the calculations such as the length of the bridge is around 700 metres and we would need 200 kilograms of sodium crumbs to sprinkle along the river bank. There was a team of 25 beggars so each one had to carry 8 kilograms of sodium with him.

We got the arrangement done for the sodium crumbs and got them packed in bags of 8 kilograms each. We were feeling like going for a mission.

"Are you sure its going to work?" I asked *Manoj.*

Manoj was certain that it was going to work for sure. We told the beggars that they are going to begin the task early that day so that they could return before the sunrise begins.

Just before returning they would manually sprinkle the sodium crumbs just at the river bank and be careful that it did not get in contact with water. *Manoj* said that it won't work if the sodium does not come in contact with water at all. I explained to him that every morning at 6 am they open the dam reservoir to let the water flow into the river. At that time the water level overflows by a few centimetres which would just be enough for the water to come in contact with the sodium which would have already been sprinkled. *Manoj* was convinced with the plan and we were about to bring the accidental epidemic to an end.

Karan said, "Sir, let's name this mission."

I think he watched too much of bollywood movies and that's why he said so. I think he was right we should name it. *Rajendra* suggested a name, "Mission ***RaKShaM***." We immediately figured it out and approved.

All was set. That night appeared so long for all of us. We were all staying at *Karan*'s place as it was the nearest to the *Sharda* bridge. We made an excuse at our homes that we were having *Manoj's* welcome party with a night out as he had come after a long gap. We hardly had anytime to sleep as we had to leave for our mission. *Karan* advised to have a quick power nap with our alarms set for 3 am sharp.

The Plan Executed

While they all were taking a nap I was thinking about *Shanaya*'s last meeting. She never called me back after she was discharged. I could not forget the last smile of gratitude that I had received from her when she was being discharged. We all had gone through disenchanting situations in the last few weeks but *Shanaya* was the only silver lining in the cloud for me. I strongly wanted this epidemic to come to an end and perhaps would never like to remember it in my life. It claimed life of innocent people. It had ruined the life of young productive citizens like *Aryan* by the impact of accidents that it had caused but *Shanaya* came with a hope for me to solve this mystery. She did not meet me for the last one decade but now that she had met perhaps because, she was sent for some purpose by the cosmos. Had she not reminded me of my own words said to her I would have never been able to find a solution to the problem.

The alarm rang and broke the silence. *Manoj* was still sleeping perhaps because his jet lag had not settled yet. We managed to wake him up with herculean efforts. *Karan*'s maid prepared tea for us and then we drove to the bridge with the sodium bags loaded in the boot of our car. I could never imagine that my capital city looks so beautiful without the disorganized traffic that we see during the day time. The roads in Delhi are wide enough and very well planned but if only our Delhiites could follow some traffic rules and possesses some road sense.

We reached the bridge within 10 minutes as there was no traffic at all. We handed over the bags to each of the beggars and their team leader instructed them what to do. The stray dogs barked at us ferociously as they saw the bags with us. We ignored them. The beggars left for the day's work and reached the bank of the river. We observed them patiently from the top of the bridge. Soon they started sprinkling the sodium crumbs along the bank of the river just the same way that we had told their team leader. I must say such an efficient team leader should be the HR of an MNC. I mean what an example of an efficient leadership to get the work done from half learned unskilled people and that too with precision. All the sodium crumbs had been sprinkled. The hooter from the dam could be heard a few minutes later as they would open the reservoir gates for the water to flow into the river. The beggars returned as soon as they heard the hooter as they knew that, that day it was going to be different. We saw a wormhole getting opened around 20 feet away from us on the bridge. It was bigger than what is was last time. While we turned to watch the wormhole our heartbeat got fast enough to give us palpitations. Perhaps it was going to be another one now.

Within no time the splash could be heard coming from the river. The whole bank of the river was enlightened with the flames of sodium formed due to the sodium crumbs coming in contact with the flowing water. The light emitted was bright enough to flash on the entire bridge. It was like a **Supernova**[8] rising from the water. As the reaction progressed the wormhole could be seen shrinking in itself. *Raju* said softly, "It is collapsing."

Karan and *Manoj* said simultaneously, "It is working, it is working."

The Supernova arising from river after the sodium reacts with water

It appeared to me that Mission *RaKSham* was accomplished or was I elated a bit earlier? Well, only time could answer it.

The wormhole collapsed within no time. Fortunately, there was no accident that morning. We were feeling victorious but only the subsequent days could tell that if we had really put that epidemic to an end.

We did not want anyone to see us so we departed for our homes before the day begins with complete sunrise.

The Last Letter

Except *Manoj* we all started our day normally at the hospital. Everyone was still talking about the incidents at *Sharda* bridge. While we listened to the conversation of the other groups carefully sometimes even overheard them deliberately.

The next few days passed but there were hardly any accidents reported from the *Sharda* bridge. Our emergency calls also reached the previous frequency of what it used to be earlier. Things seemed to be normalizing by then. *Barbara Brown* was also discharged from *Karan*'s Hospital by then. *Manoj* was all set to return to the US.

Raju pointed out that I had not got my white overcoat washed for the last one week as it was looking dirty. While I was taking it off I saw a piece of paper folded and kept in the top left pocket. I opened it and it left me in tears:

Dear Doc

If you are reading this letter right now then it means you are safe and have terminated the accidental epidemic. I knew only you could do it perhaps that's why I could trust no one but you. Victor, myself and my son met with an accident in this accidental epidemic a few days before I met you. My son and Victor did not survive. I managed to survive but when I woke up, I opened my eyes in another dimension in another time. Perhaps that is the beginning of a new life for me in another dimension. Barbara Brown had come to attend my condolence meeting itself. That is because I went missing so everyone in my family concluded that I am no more. I had a strong desire to meet you before I died but I thought that it would be left unfulfilled. The dimension of the universe that I am currently in has developed a technological device to travel to another dimension. The cell phone like device that I concealed from you, when u came to meet me in my ward room, was that inter-dimensional travel device itself. It is known as the **LINK** *over here. I am currently stuck in this dimension that has a cutting edge technology but no family, no friends and certainly not YOU either.*

Samrat reading Shanaya's last letter

I never spoke to Victor while I was admitted in the city hospital. I only pretended to do so. In fact, it was no one but me who was replying to the constable Yadav Ji's messages from Victor's cell phone. Our driver whom you met was unaware of our accident as he was in his village for his daughter's marriage at that time. He was supposed to return the same day when I was brought to the casualty of the City Hospital. So I called my driver from Victor's cell phone to make things look normal.

I decided to come back to your dimension and meet you but your current time is still not prepared to accommodate a travel to another dimension. In fact, it became an untimely accidental epidemic. I wanted to stay in your current time but now this body of mine can with stand another dimension for not more than a week. After that it would have become mere ashes. I am happy that you saved the mankind from this havoc. I could have taken yourself with me but your body cannot withstand my current dimension either. Moreover, I did not want Chandani to be left alone, jokes apart doc. I am now aware of the exact time when we shall be together once again but the cosmos principles prohibit me to disclose the future of any dimension to anyone. The future of one dimension in the universe could be the present or the past for another. I am patiently waiting for you in this dimension and will continue to do so until we meet again. Time can keep us distant but not apart.

Yours only
Shanaya

This accidental epidemic transformed me and my friends completely. We were no longer the same human beings anymore. We felt elated and honoured. No one would perhaps ever recognize us for what we had done but the world's biggest recognition of one's self is into the mirror. If you can say in front of a mirror, that's the man I want myself to be, then you have given a meaning to your life. The life we live is given to us with some purpose by the cosmos. Once we meet that purpose that we are sent for, we can proudly look at ourselves and inspire thousands others to serve their respective ones. A man is borned twice in his life; once on his birthday and second on the day he realizes the purpose of his very existence. Life is not about reaching a destination but the journey one goes through. The destination is the same for all of us but what matters is how has one lived up his journey in order to reach that destination.

With time passing, the human race is becoming more and more ambitious but less ethical. Ambitions should always be high on one hand but with ethics to serve the mankind on another, can only add meaning to the tasks done by us on any platform provided to us.

Any untoward event occurring in the society has a direct or indirect correlation with us which will affect us in some form or another, if not today then tomorrow. Hence, be responsible and be receptive. Don't be an ostrich to close eyes to any wrong taking place around us. Don't react but respond with your intellect to find a solution to the problem around you.

As the solution often lies in the problem itself.

Epilogue

So what happens to *Shanaya* after this? How long will *Shanaya* wait to meet *Samrat* again? Will *Samrat* marry *Chandani* by then? It might be that *Samrat* will now make an effort to search for *Shanaya* in some other dimension. Will he ever have an access to the technological device called The LINK? May be *Manoj* can help him develop such a device. A device like LINK can bring a revolution for the mankind if used judiciously and honestly. Who was the lady with the pram who crossed *Samrat's* car on the *Sharda* Bridge?

Shanaya left with the driver when she was being discharged from the hospital. Did she ever sit in the car driven by her driver? Perhaps she only pretended to go out and left for her dimension using the LINK.

There seems many possibilities but then let's see what happens in the next sequel.

ððð

Glossary

Pg No.	Term	Definition
48	Space-time grid[1]	It is a mathematical model that fuses the multiple dimensions of space and the one dimension of time on a graph
50	Wormhole[2]	A tunnel like pathway connecting 2 different points in the universe
54	Time Dilation[3]	A phenomenon in which when an object is moving very fast it experiences time more slowly than when it is stationary
59	Etiology[4]	The cause or origin of disease.
60	Negative Mass[5]	An object with an opposite gravitational pull i.e instead of attracting objects it throws them away from itself
64	Superfluid[6]	A fluid capable of flowing freely without any restriction in any direction
64	Absolute Zero[7]	It is the lowest possible temperature
71	Supernova[8]	The illumination created due to the explosion of a star in the universe